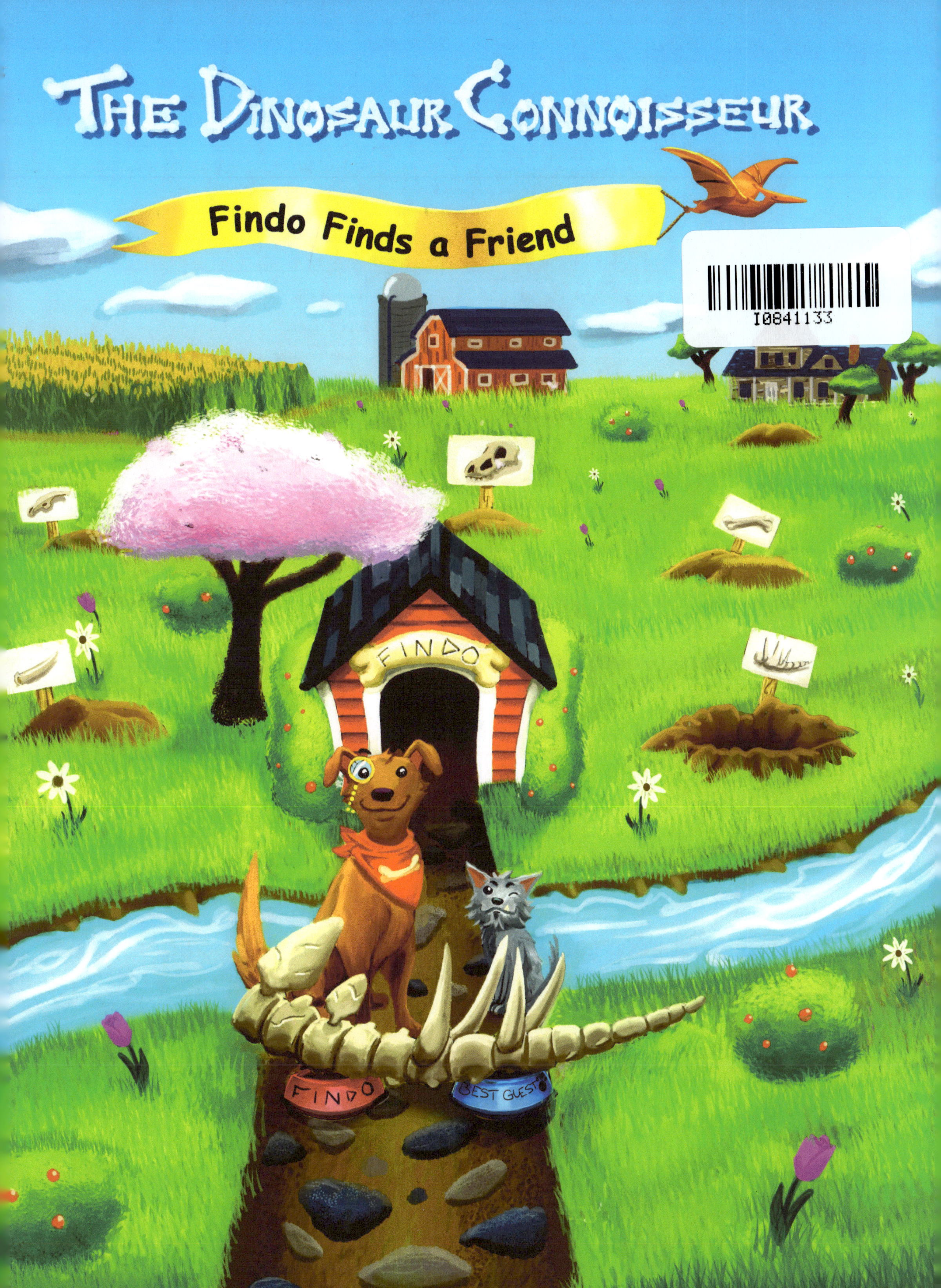
THE DINOSAUR CONNOISSEUR
Findo Finds a Friend
FINDO
FINDO
BEST GUEST

THE DINOSAUR CONNOISSEUR
FINDO FINDS A FRIEND

Written by Charles Shook
Illustrated by Andre Trowel, Jr
Library of Congress Cataloging-in-Publication Data is avaliable
Printed in the United States of America

First Edition: November 2021

I wrote this book for my nephew.
I hope you like it, too.

If you really do,
I will write more for you.

The Dinosaur Connoisseur went out to find a bone.

He dug down deep,
then went to sleep,
and dreamed he was
at home.
FINDO

He slept all night
beneath the stars,

far away from passing cars.

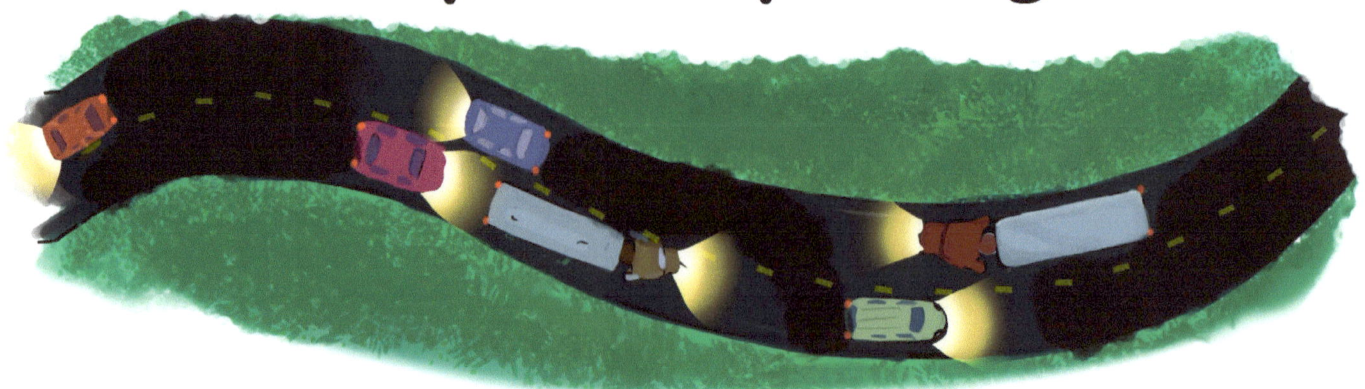

He slept until the sun
was high,
then woke with a throat
sore and dry.

He dug some more until he found a treasure buried underground.

It looked so GOOD!
He licked his chops!

The big horn of a
TRICERATOPS!

He took it home
and washed and cleaned,

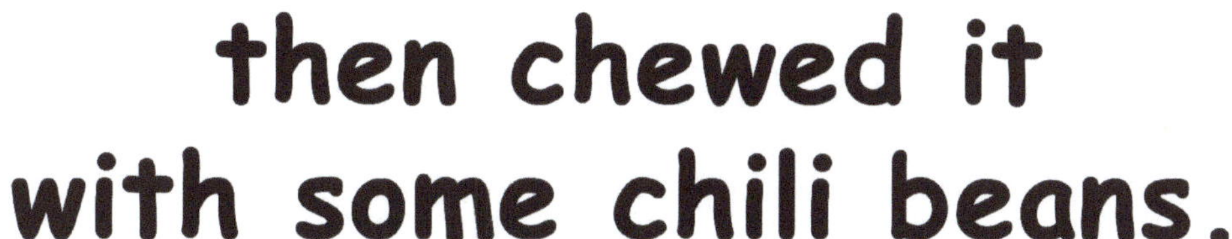

then chewed it
with some chili beans.

He said,"WOW! This bone's a winner!
I'll save some for tomorrow's dinner."

So he took the horn to the back yard,
and dug down deep with claws so hard,

then buried it the same way he found,
way down deep under the ground.

As he buried,
a stranger passed by
who sat and watched
with a question in his eyes.

Findo noticed him and said, "What is it you'd like to ask, my friend?"

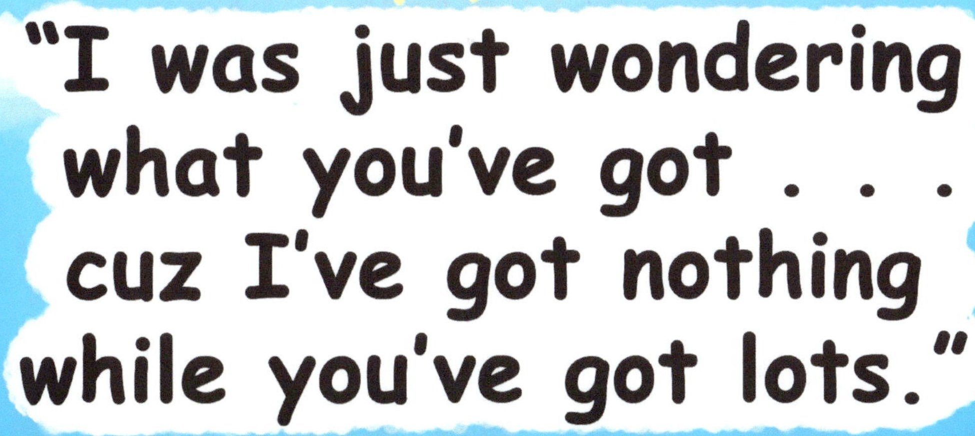
"I was just wondering
what you've got . . .
cuz I've got nothing
while you've got lots."

"I smell bones on the wind in every direction. The ones from dinosaurs are aged to perfection."
FIDO

"I'll dig you up any bone you'd like,"

and serve it to you
in my best guest pail.

I bet you'd love
a stegosaurus' tail!"

"Thanks so much!
This bone is delicious!
After I eat,

I'll wash the dishes...

to show my appreciation for how you shared."
"Of course, that's how we show we care."

Besides, bones taste even better
when we break them together."

Thank You For Reading!